Alice's Shooting Star

Alice's Shooting Star

Written by

Tim Kennemore

Illustrated by

Mike Spoor

First published 2005 by Andersen Press Ltd,
20 Vauxhall Bridge Road
London SW1V 2SA, England

This edition published 2009 by
Eerdmans Books for Young Readers,
an imprint of Wm. B. Eerdmans Publishing Co.

Wm. B. Eerdmans Publishing Co.
2140 Oak Industrial Dr. NE, Grand Rapids, Michigan 49505
P.O. Box 163, Cambridge CB3 9PU U.K.
www.eerdmans.com/youngreaders

Printed in the United States of America

09 10 11 12   8 7 6 5 4 3 2 1

Library of Congress Cataloging-in-Publication Data

Kennemore, Tim.
Alice's shooting star / Tim Kennemore; illustrated by Mike Spoor.
p.   cm.
Summary: Middle sister Alice helps her family recognize that her exuberant
younger sister Rosie's accounts of her day are cre⬛⬛⬛⬛⬛⬛⬛ er han lies.
ISBN 978-0-8⬛
[1. Imagination — Fi⬛
3. Family li⬛

Contents

1

Sonic the Batflap

Alice Singer was eight and a half, and life was good. She enjoyed school nearly all the time, and she had three special friends, Sophie, Natasha, and May. All three loved being invited to her house, because her mom and dad were so easy to be around. They liked to joke and laugh, and always knew how to make a guest feel at home. Alice had an adorable guinea pig and a bedroom packed full of books and toys and games. She knew she had nothing to complain about.

And yet, sometimes she felt so very ordinary. She was just exactly average in every way a child could be. She had mid-length, mid-brown hair with a slight curl, and greeny-brown eyes that people called hazel. She was precisely the average height and weight for her age, and sometimes she felt that in a crowd she more or less disappeared.

And, of course, she was the middle one of three children.

Her brother Oliver was the oldest, the tallest, and the cleverest. In fact, Oliver was even older, taller, and more clever than people of his own age, so it was clear that Alice would never catch up to him in any way. It might sound strange to say that someone was older than people of his own age, but anyone who knew Oliver would understand perfectly. He was a chess champion, he was the second best in his entire grade at math, and he had won the school's Tidiness Award three years in a row.

But even Oliver somehow paled into nothingness beside their little sister Rosie. Rosie was quite spectacularly unusual. She was so famous that more people at Alice's school knew Rosie than knew Alice. Alice had been there for three years, and Rosie wasn't even starting until next September!

Rosie was such a genius at causing trouble

that she got herself thrown out of two day care centers before she was three years old. She had by now been at the Humpty Dumpty Day Care for eighteen months. They had very nearly thrown her out after the last Christmas Nativity play, but Rosie was skilled at covering her tracks. Everyone was certain that she had been responsible for the many disasters that befell that play, but nothing could ever be proven.

So Rosie was given one last chance. And since then, to everyone's great surprise, she had become quite good. For days on end she acted almost like a regular person. And all this time, as she learned more and more words, she was developing a brand new talent — a talent that seemed to have passed Alice by altogether. Rosie had a fabulous and colorful imagination.

"I'm taller than Oliver now!" she would say to Grandma Singer on the telephone, although Oliver was eleven and Rosie was only four. "Yes I am. I growed yesterday."

"We had a new little girl at school today!" she would say. "What was her name?" Alice asked, suspiciously, and "Sticky Bun," said Rosie. According to Rosie, new children were arriving at Humpty Dumpty every week. There were little girls called Rainbow Polly, Fluffy, and Strawberry Smoothie. There were little boys named Rover, Grimble, and Sonic the Batflap. They all played together with angelfish and spider dragons, and after story time they went up in a purple spaceship to the moon.

For some reason Mom and Dad didn't appreciate Rosie's gift for imagination. They called it "lying."

But Alice was fascinated by the way magic words came flowing out of her sister's mouth like a sparkling river of pure nonsense. She bought a small orange notebook and began to take notes. For one whole week she wrote down Rosie's version of the lunch menu at Humpty Dumpty. It went like this:

Monday: Fish fingers, raisins and toast, barbecue beef monster munchies, sparklefruit, and fishy bamana. (Rosie could not say the word "banana" properly. She could say it wrong in all sorts of different ways, but she could not say it right.)

Tuesday: Fish pie, Christmas pudding, magic starcake, and a Pick and Mix bag.

Wednesday: Green ginger goodie things, pork and glitterberries, and chicken in a basket.

Thursday: Rosie wasn't allowed to say what she had had for lunch because a policeman had come and told all the children it was a secret.

Friday: Sausages, tulipfish, and lemon fried toasty doughnut pudding.

On Friday when the list was complete, Alice showed it to Rosie.

"Yes, that's right," said Rosie, nodding, although she couldn't read.

"The green ginger goodie things you had on Wednesday, were they fish?" asked Alice.

"We aren't allowed fish on Wednesdays," said Rosie sternly, and disappeared into the backyard.

"You shouldn't pretend to believe her," said Oliver. "She'll never learn to tell the truth if you do."

"Oliver's right, Alice," said Dad. "We're all going to have to be stricter, before it's too late."

"But it isn't like bad lying," said Alice. "She doesn't tell lies to get herself out of trouble. She just pretends things are more interesting than they really are."

"She *does* tell lies to get out of trouble when she wants to," said Mom. "When she doesn't bother, it's because she *likes* trouble."

"And think about this, Alice," said Dad. "If Rosie wandered off and got lost, and a policeman found her and asked her name and address, it wouldn't be much help if she said her name was Pepperoni Pizza and she lived in a magic windmill in Munchkinland, would it?"

"By the time Rosie had finished with the policeman, they'd be riding across the sea together on the back of a giant turtle to the edge of the world, eating pink licorice pudding and fish," said Alice. She was rather proud of this. It sounded almost as good as something Rosie would say. Alice's teacher at school was always telling her that her stories would be better if she used her imagination more.

But Alice's brain didn't work that way. She

wrote ordinary stories about ordinary children doing things in the real world. They were deadly dull, but it was the only sort of story she seemed able to manage. She had tried to write stories about witches and wizards, with a magic shell that told you a secret password when you held it against your ear. She had started a story about an invisible dog called Spotless. But none of these stories ever came out the way she hoped. Alice's mind didn't work the right way. Perhaps if she spent more time listening to Rosie, she would learn how it was done.

But Mom and Dad and Oliver were all shaking their heads.

"I thought you were old enough to be sensible about this, Alice," said Mom. "It's not a joking matter."

Alice sighed. She knew what that meant. It meant that it was okay for her mom or dad to make a joke about it, but not for Alice. They did this sometimes. They pretended they were treating her like a grown-up, but they weren't really.

"I shall try to teach Rosie to tell the truth,"

said Oliver. Oliver had never made a joke in his life as far as Alice could remember, and so was never in danger of making one at the wrong time.

"Thank you, Oliver," said Mom.

Alice raised her eyebrows. This would be very interesting indeed.

2

Good as Gold

Alice thought her parents were making a big mistake. Rosie's storytelling seemed to use up that part of her attention that had previously been devoted to causing mayhem. Take the lies away from her and anything might happen.

And the lies were so much more fun than anything she had ever done before.

Until Rosie was one and a half, all she had done was scream. She had screamed all day and all night. She screamed in her sleep. She screamed while she was being fed, which caused an incredible mess. You could still see the splash marks on the walls. Throughout this time Mom and Dad had gone around looking like ghosts with huge dark circles under their eyes. They would fall asleep at the dinner table, until woken by another piercing yell from Rosie.

So nobody who had lived through it would ever, ever forget Rosie as a baby. As for Oliver, he had been the first baby of the family, and so nobody would ever forget him either. The first baby is always the most important. There were at least three hundred photographs of baby Oliver. By the time Alice came along, her parents weren't so interested in photographs anymore. There weren't half as many photos of baby Alice, and most of them had Oliver in them as well, looking perfect in proper clothes, while Alice lolled around, small and bald and helpless, in a pink romper. Alice sometimes thought that her entire babyhood had been lost in everyone's memory.

"What was I like when I was a baby?" she asked Mom.

"Oh, you were as good as gold!" said her mother, with a warm sappy smile.

This wasn't what Alice had hoped to hear.

"But did I do anything interesting?" she asked.

Her mother thought for a moment. "Yes!" she said.

Alice perked up. "What?"

"You used to sit and look out of the window for hours and hours!" Mom said proudly. "Just sitting there by yourself, thinking. Everyone thought it was quite remarkable!"

Alice sighed and gave up. At the age when Oliver had been crawling around his room with a ruler to make sure all his toys were placed exactly nine inches apart, the age when Rosie had already been plotting her first explosion of the garden shed, what had Alice been doing? *Looking out of the window!* No wonder nobody remembered her. She must have been the most boring baby in the history of the universe.

When Rosie was two, and only screaming about half the time, she suddenly decided to talk. They were all out together in town when Rosie noticed a large blue swing set in the toy store window. It had a slide, a swing, and a rope ladder.

"I want that," said Rosie.

Everyone stood frozen in amazement.

"I want that," said Rosie again.

"Am I dreaming," said Mom, "or was that Rosie talking?"

Rosie bounced up and down in her stroller and waved her fat little arms hopefully towards the store window.

"Rosie!" said Alice. "You can talk!" She couldn't believe it. At last Rosie was starting to be a person. She squatted down by the stroller and took her hand. "Hello, Rosie. Do you know who I am? Do you know my name?"

"I WANT THAT," said Rosie, snatching her hand away from Alice and pointing at the swing set.

"But darling, it's a hundred and fifty dollars!" said Mom.

"We can't possibly afford it," said Dad. "Rosie, would you like a bouncy ball?"

Rosie screamed for the rest of the day, and she didn't say anything else for another six months.

Alice was very disappointed. In the intervening

months, she had spent hours with Rosie, trying to persuade her to say something — anything, even to say, "Go away, Alice." But it was no use. Rosie just glared at her darkly, as if to say, "Well, I tried talking, and it didn't work."

So you wouldn't hear Alice complain about Rosie's stories. Rosie had been completely useless as company for nearly her whole life so far, and now all of a sudden she had become interesting. And it was stupid, what her dad had said about Rosie getting lost and telling the policeman her name was Pepperoni Pizza. Rosie's lies couldn't possibly be mistaken for the truth. If Rosie said, "My name is Lucy Loggins and I live at 43 Pinetree Drive," well, *then* you could see that there might be a problem. The policeman would take Rosie to Pinetree Drive and expect the people there to be thrilled to see their little Lucy safely returned to them, and there would be all kinds of confusion. But as it was, the policeman would just take Rosie to the police station and wait until someone came to get her. Probably her mom and dad would be at the

police station before Rosie and the policeman even got there.

So there was no problem at all.

3

Middle-sized Brown Boxes

Oliver thought very seriously about how he was going to teach Rosie to tell the truth. In the end, he decided that she simply didn't understand what telling the truth actually meant. Oliver would explain. And he would explain with the help of his collection of boxes.

Oliver had been collecting boxes for as long as Alice could remember. Nobody really understood why. There were hundreds of boxes in his room, stacked under the bed, on the dresser, and in tidy piles up against the wall. There wasn't anything in them except more boxes. Some of the larger boxes had neat little labels on them saying things like, "Middle-sized brown boxes (hinged lid)" and some of the middle-sized boxes had neat little labels saying things like, "Small rectangular boxes (no top)."

Alice had tried asking him about them but didn't get very far.

"One day I might need a box," said Oliver.

"What for?" said Alice.

"To put things in," said Oliver patiently. "One day you might need a box, Alice, and you'll find you don't have one."

Alice couldn't see this presenting much of a problem, not in their house.

"I'll borrow one of yours," she said.

"You certainly will not," said Oliver, horrified. "You might damage it."

So it was all very surprising when Oliver brought three boxes downstairs and put them on the kitchen table ready for Rosie's lesson.

Everyone gathered around to watch.

"Now Rosie," said Oliver, looking down at her in a very grown-up way. "You see these three boxes?"

Rosie nodded.

"One is big and grey. One is small and red. And this one here is middle-sized and green."

Rosie nodded.

"Now, I am going to teach you to tell the truth. If you do, you can choose one of the boxes to keep!"

Alice was amazed. Oliver had never been known to part with one of his boxes.

"Don't want a box," said Rosie. "Boxes are stupid. Want a car."

Oliver ignored this. Rosie was obviously lying again. How could anybody not want a box?

"This box is grey," he said, pointing to the big grey box. "So when I say this box is grey, I am telling the truth. Do you understand, Rosie?"

Rosie cupped her chin in her hands and leaned on her elbows and raised her eyes to heaven. Oliver picked up the red box.

"This little box is red," he said. "If I said this box was yellow, I would be telling a lie. Do you understand, Rosie?"

Rosie stuck her fingers in her ears and wiggled

19

her nose. Oliver picked up the middle-sized green box.

"Telling lies is wrong," said Oliver. "You must always tell the truth, Rosie. The truth is that this box is green."

Rosie blew out her cheeks and smacked them — *pop!* Oliver handed her the little red box. Rosie made a face.

"Now," said Oliver, rather like a magician who is finally ready to pull the rabbit out of the hat. "What color is the box in your hand, Rosie?"

Rosie looked down at the box with a very bored face as if she didn't much care, thought for a few seconds, and said, "Thursday."

"Don't be ridiculous, Rosie," said Oliver. The tips of his ears began to turn pink. "You can't answer that question with 'Thursday.' It doesn't make sense."

Rosie gave him a long, hard look, as if to say, "It is a perfectly good answer. You just asked the wrong question."

She put the little red box back on the table and looked around. Mom and Dad and Alice were

all standing in a row, waiting to see what would happen next.

"Oliver is annoying me," said Rosie. And with that, she got up and left the room.

"I'm going to put her to bed," said Mom. "Rosie! It's nearly seven-thirty. Bedtime!"

It was in fact only about fourteen minutes after seven, but Alice's mom and dad were not above telling lies themselves when it came to getting Rosie to bed. Her actual bedtime was supposed to be seven-thirty, but in their anxiety for some peace and quiet they were capable of stretching the word "nearly" quite a bit. Fortunately, Rosie couldn't tell time, and at this rate she was never likely to learn how. She would grow up thinking that when the big hand was anywhere between the twelve and the five, it was "nearly half past." But grown-ups, of course, were allowed to tell lies when they wanted to.

*   *   *

After the affair with the boxes, Oliver announced that he had given up on Rosie and that he wasn't going to bother with her again until she was a proper person. "I won't try to help her with anything again for another twenty years," he said sniffily. He took his boxes back upstairs and spent the rest of the day rearranging them into different stacks and piles.

"Eighty-nine years, please," said Rosie, when she heard.

Alice's mom and dad put their heads together and made a plan of their own to teach Rosie not to tell lies. They drew up a chart with felt pens on a huge piece of paper that Mom brought back from the office where she worked. At the top of the paper the words ROSIE'S TRUTH-TELLING STAR CHART were written in red and purple capital letters. Underneath this they had drawn thick black horizontal lines. Every line was divided up into boxes, one for each day of the week, for Monday to Friday.

"Every day you tell the truth about what happened at Humpty Dumpty," said Mom to Rosie, "you get a big gold star!" She produced a little box full of sticky gold stars.

"Oooh!" said Rosie.

"And every day you tell lies" — out came another box — "you get a big black blob!"

"Oooh!" said Rosie. "Big black blob!"

"And if you get five gold stars in a row," said Dad, "we will give you one dollar to put in your piggy bank."

"Big black blob!" said Rosie dreamily. She reached over for the box of sticky black blobs and gazed at them in wonder.

Alice could already picture the lines of big black blobs going across the chart, and Rosie gazing at them with as much happiness as if she had won the lottery. This was not going to work. None of them understood Rosie at all.

4

Hollyflower

The next week was a very lively one at Humpty Dumpty.

According to Rosie, the following things happened:

On Monday, there was a new girl named Hollyflower.

On Tuesday, Rosie painted two of the children, Toby and Jessica, with pink and purple stripes, and then covered them all over with glue and silver stars.

On Wednesday, a lady lollipop called Strawberry came to see the children and told them lots of secrets.

On Thursday, Amanda told them that instead of having a Christmas Nativity Play this year, they were all going to be fruits and vegetables instead.

And on Friday, they had fishy cake for lunch.

Alice's mom sighed at this last piece of news, went over to Rosie's Truth-Telling Star Chart, and added the fifth in the first row of big black blobs. A whole weekful.

"Bingo!" thought Alice. Rosie beamed.

"Now," said Mom to Rosie, "tell us what you really had for lunch. Was it chocolate cake? Fruit cake? Not cake at all?"

"Fishy cake," said Rosie.

Suddenly, Alice had an idea. "What color was the fishy cake, Rosie?" she asked.

Rosie thought for a while and said, "Orange."

"She's completely hopeless," said Oliver, looking up from the book he was reading, which was called *Trainspotting for Beginners.* "You really mustn't encourage her, Alice."

Alice ignored this. "And what color was it inside?" she asked.

"Fishy white!" said Rosie.

"Mom," said Alice, "she had fish sticks! Like we get from the grocery store!"

There was a silence while everyone thought about this.

"Goodness," said Mom at last. "You're right, Alice. I'm sorry, Rosie, really I am. But you've told us such strange things about fish and puddings over the months, you can see the way my mind went."

"No need for the big black blob!" said Dad.

"No!" said Mom, and she went back to the chart, peeled the blob off, and threw it in the trash. "You can have a beautiful gold star instead! Well done."

Rosie looked horrified.

*   *   *

The next day, Saturday, something even more surprising happened. They were all sitting around after breakfast deciding what to do next, when the phone rang. Alice's mom went out into the hall to answer it. When she came back, she

had the most peculiar expression on her face. She looked as if she was trying very hard not to laugh, and she was gazing over at Rosie's chart in a puzzled, thoughtful sort of way.

"You'll never guess who that was," she said.

"You'd better tell us, then," said Dad.

"That was Mrs. Fowler," said Mom.

"Who?" said Dad. Oliver, who had looked up briefly from *Trainspotting for Beginners,* looked down again; nobody called Mrs. Fowler could possibly be of interest to him.

"She called to ask if Rosie would like to come and play," said Mom.

"She wants to play with Rosie?" said Dad. "Is the woman crazy?"

"No! To play with her daughter, who started at Humpty Dumpty on Monday. Apparently she and Rosie are the very best of friends."

Everyone looked stunned. Rosie didn't have friends. She had victims.

"And her daughter's name," said Mom, "is Holly. Holly Fowler."

"Hollyflower!" said Rosie, triumphantly.

Another black blob was taken down and re-placed by a gold star.

Rosie looked aghast.

Alice's mom and dad agreed that it would be safer if Holly Fowler came to their house to play with Rosie, so they could keep an eye on things. You couldn't really expect Mrs. Fowler to realize quite how many eyes would be necessary.

Mrs. Fowler and Holly arrived twenty minutes later. Alice went to answer the door and let them in. "Hello, Mrs. Fowler," she said politely. "Mom says to please come in and have a cup of coffee. Hello, Holly."

Holly made a tiny high-pitched squeaking noise. Alice looked down at her from what sud-denly seemed like a very great height. Holly Fowler was one of the smallest children she had ever seen in her life. She looked as if you could fold her up and put her in a baby stroller and her feet wouldn't even stick out over the edge. She looked like a doll. She looked as if Rosie could eat her for lunch.

"Hello, Pollyanna," said Mrs. Fowler to Alice. "How nice to meet you! Rosie has told Holly all about her big sister. I'm glad to see you're out of the hospital already."

"Um . . . you'd better come on in," said Alice in desperation, and stood back to let Mrs. Fowler and Holly lead the way into the kitchen.

"Hollyflower!" cried Rosie, joyfully.

"Hello, Rosie!" squeaked Hollyflower.

"Hello, everyone!" said Mrs. Fowler. "You must be Rosie's mom and dad. Holly, say hello!" Holly squeaked something indistinguishable. "And this," she turned to Oliver, "must be Pugsley. What an interesting name, dear! I hear you're quite a whiz on the electric guitar."

Oliver's jaw dropped in amazement.

Alice decided that this would be a very good time to slip upstairs and spend quite a long time washing her hands and brushing her teeth.

5

Strawberry the Lady Lollipop

When Alice went back down to the kitchen, Dad and Oliver had gotten the new video camera out, Rosie and Hollyflower were sitting on the floor in the corner whispering to each other, and Mom and Mrs. Fowler were drinking coffee. Mrs. Fowler looked as if she needed it. She kept glancing over at Rosie in a very nervous sort of way. She was starting to learn.

"Sorry, Alice," Mrs. Fowler said. "I thought . . . Holly said . . ."

"It's all right," said Alice.

"Come on, Hollyflower," said Rosie, all of a sudden jumping to her feet. "Time to go out and play Mrs. Strawberry Lady Lollipop."

They raced out to the backyard. Alice, Oliver,

and the grown-ups watched through the kitchen window.

"I'll take some video of them playing," Dad said, getting to his feet.

"Me too," said Oliver. "I need to practice."

Mom gave a muffled snort. Their old video camera had died about a year earlier. It had survived a great deal, but it could not survive Rosie teaching it to swim. The new one was about a quarter as big, and, as Mom never tired of pointing out, it had cost a fortune. Dad and Oliver were forever cooing over it and fiddling around with the settings.

"Boys and their toys!" Mom would grumble.

Alice didn't like the sound of that. Toys should be for everybody. It was true that Mom didn't seem to have much time for toys any more. But Alice wasn't going to grow up to be like that. She would always have toys. She would buy wonderful grown-up toys. She would have a video camera, a computer so tiny it fit into your hand, video game machines and pinball machines, a portable music player and a robot dog, and she

33

would never ever say to her own children, "Boys and their toys!"

Dad and Oliver went outside to videotape Rosie and Hollyflower. It was hard to tell exactly what was happening, but it seemed to involve Rosie marching around carrying a broom upside down and giving orders, while Hollyflower scuttled obediently behind.

Alice had a flash of inspiration. "Got it!" she said.

"Got what?" asked Mom.

"The lady lollipop called Strawberry," said Alice. "The one Rosie told us about on Wednesday, and you gave her a big black blob."

"Yes?" said Mom.

"It *was* a lollipop lady!" said Alice. "That's what the kids call the woman who holds up the stop sign and helps them cross the street."

"That's right," agreed Mrs. Fowler. "A crossing guard did visit the school on Wednesday to teach the children a bit about road safety. She was still there when I picked up Holly, and we had a lovely chat. I think her name was Mrs. Stowerbury."

"Strawberry the lady lollipop!" said Alice.

"Oh dear," said Mom.

Now there were only two black blobs left on Rosie's chart. The other three had turned into gold stars.

Dad came back indoors, leaving Oliver to finish the video, and stopped when he saw the chart. Alice explained what had happened.

"I've got a bad feeling about this," said Dad, still looking at the blobs. "Can I ask you what might sound like a very silly question, Maxine?"

Maxine was Mrs. Fowler. They had all swapped first names while Alice was upstairs. Alice never knew whether this meant her too. Some grown-ups liked you to call them by their first names and some didn't, and you never really knew which was which, or why, until you got it wrong. There didn't seem to be any sensible rules. At Rosie's day care, the children were only three or four years old, but they all called the teachers Amanda and Carol and Juliet. At Oliver's school, some of the children were completely grown up, but they still had to call the teachers Mr. and Mrs.

and Miss. The woman who ran the newspaper shop was called Mrs. Pocock, but the man who came to clean their windows once a month, who was years and years older than Mrs. Pocock, was called Bill. Alice thought that Mrs. Fowler was probably a Mrs. Fowler by the look of her, but she couldn't be sure.

"Ask away," said Mrs. Fowler to Dad.

Alice had been so busy wondering what she was supposed to call Mrs. Fowler that she had quite forgotten that Dad was going to ask a silly question.

"You wouldn't by any chance have heard anything about this year's Nativity Play?" he asked.

"Why, yes!" said Mrs. Fowler. "They aren't going to have one, in the traditional sense anyway. I was talking to Amanda about it only yesterday." Amanda was the head of Humpty Dumpty. "Apparently last year some child managed to persuade the three kings that because the inn was full and there wasn't any food for the baby Jesus, at the end of the play all three of them would be eaten. And that the gold and frankincense and myrrh were special sauces for them to be cooked in. And they just weren't able to carry on. I mean, you wouldn't, would you? What sort of a child would think up a terrible lie like that?"

Mom and Dad wriggled uncomfortably and tried very hard not to look out towards the backyard, where Rosie was riding on the broom like a witch, with Holly still trotting along behind.

"And then," Mrs. Fowler went on, "someone pushed the angel on the end and they all of them toppled over like a row of dominoes!"

"No!" said Dad.

"Mary was very nearly strangled by her own halo, the shepherds started a lamb fight, and the baby Jesus's head fell off. I'm not surprised that they didn't want to try it again."

"No," said Mom faintly. Outside, Rosie was busy digging a very large hole. Alice began to wonder if it was entirely wise to be taping video evidence of all this.

"So this year they're all dressing up as fruits and vegetables and singing Christmas songs," said Mrs. Fowler. "Carol's been working on the

costumes for months already. It sounds a lot safer to me. In my opinion, there's a limit to the damage that even the worst-behaved little boy can do, if you dress him up as a tomato."

"Boy?" said Dad.

"Well, it must have been a boy," said Mrs. Fowler. "It's always the boys, isn't it? They're always the badly behaved ones. I'm so glad Holly has found a nice little friend like Rosie." It was impossible not to notice that out in the yard Hollyflower was now standing against the wall with an apple on her head, looking worried.

"Er . . . yes," said Mom weakly.

"Anyway," said Mrs. Fowler, "they sent out a note about it yesterday, so Rosie probably has it in her school bag."

Alice went off to find Rosie's bag. Mrs. Fowler was amazing. Holly had only been at Humpty Dumpty for a week, and Rosie had been there for a year and a half. And yet Mrs. Fowler already knew absolutely everything that had ever happened at Humpty Dumpty. She knew more than Mom and Dad did. Alice could see how that had happened. Mrs. Fowler was one of those women who would just stand and talk and talk and talk for hours. And Carol, who was one of the teachers at Humpty Dumpty, was exactly the same. Poor Holly probably had to stand around for half an hour at the end of every day waiting to go home. Alice had always been very glad her mom wasn't like that. Dads, on the whole, never seemed to be like that, although Alice didn't know as many dads as moms.

She found Rosie's bag stuffed behind the couch in the living room. There was indeed a note inside it about the Nativity Play that wasn't going to be a Nativity Play. And there was something else. The answer to the last mystery of the black blobs.

6

Big Black Blobs

"Look what I found!" said Alice, racing back into the kitchen. "You remember why Rosie got her blob on Tuesday?"

"I was just thinking about that," said Dad. "It seems to be the only one left."

"Didn't she say she'd painted two of the children all over and covered them with glue?" said Mom.

"Almost," said Alice. "She said she painted Toby and Jessica in pink and purple stripes and covered them with glue and silver stars. And look at this!" She pulled a large, rolled-up picture out of Rosie's bag and laid it out on the table.

The picture was not something you would easily forget. It looked like two huge purple and pink striped balloons, over which somebody had tipped a pot of glue and hundreds of silver stars. At the bottom one of the teachers had printed: "Toby and Jessica, by Rosie."

"That's right," said Mrs. Fowler. "They did do portraits on Tuesday. Holly did a very sweet painting of Rosie. We've pinned it up on the bulletin board in our kitchen."

Everyone looked at Rosie's picture.

"I don't think I could quite live with that in the kitchen," said Dad.

Mom went over and called Rosie and Holly inside.

"I was the big boss witch and Hollyflower was the baby witch," said Rosie. "When the dragon comes, he eats the baby witch first. So the big witch digged a big hole and buried the baby witch, and then she went home for her supper."

Hollyflower made a nervous little squeak.

"Rosie," said Mom, "I'm so sorry. Everything we gave you a big black blob for was true, all the time! I'm just going to take the last blob down and give you a gold star instead."

Rosie looked appalled.

"Big black blobs!" she said.

"All gone!" said Mom.

"And you can have a whole dollar to put in your piggy bank!" said Dad.

"Big black blobs gone!" said Holly. Rosie gave her a dark look, as if to say, "I'll deal with you later."

"You really did paint Toby and Jessica," said Dad. "And you did have fishy cake, and there was a lollipop lady, and there really is a Hollyflower!"

"And it was even true about the Nativity Play," said Mom.

"All the angels went BANG CRASH!" said Rosie, lost in a happy memory.

Mrs. Fowler gave Rosie a strange look.

"Have some more coffee!" said Mom.

"BANG CRASH in a pile!" said Rosie.

Mrs. Fowler was looking very worried indeed.

*　　*　　*

Alice's mom and dad were very pleased with the effect of Rosie's truth-telling chart and were constantly admiring the row of gold stars. They gave Rosie four quarters, which she put in her piggy bank without much interest. Money didn't mean a great deal to Rosie.

None of this seemed right to Alice. Rosie was being paid to tell the truth, which was something Alice did all the time, and nobody gave her any money. And Rosie might be telling the truth about what she had done at Humpty Dumpty that day, but it didn't stop her from telling the most awful whoppers at other times, particularly to Hollyflower. Hollyflower, who lived one street over, was becoming a regular visitor, and Rosie told her the most dreadful tales.

"There's a secret room at Humpty Dumpty where the naughty children are put, Hollyflower," she would say, "and the Easter egg monster turns them into chocolate rabbits, and they never see their families ever again!" Hollyflower's eyes would grow huge and round with terror. She was too frightened even to squeak. But somehow she kept coming back for more.

Alice watched all this in bewilderment. She

decided in the end that Holly was the same as people who liked to watch horror movies. They were scared, but at the same time they enjoyed being scared. And they knew that really it was just pretend. When Holly grew up, she would probably spend all her time watching movies like *Slimy Swamp Thing with Two Heads* and *Frankenstein's Monster Ate My Mother.* Only none of them would ever be as good as Rosie.

Dinner became very dull.

"We had sausages, peas, and mashed potatoes for lunch," Rosie would say. Alice was bored. She thought back sadly to the good old days of curried pig, fishy ice cream, and daffodilburgers. Every day at Humpty Dumpty the children did coloring, sang songs, had drinks and cookies, and listened to a story. It all sounded so incredibly dull that you could hardly blame Rosie for inventing something more interesting. But her parents thought it was wonderful.

"Well done, Rosie!" said Mom.

"Excellent!" said Dad. "Another gold star!"

Rosie glared darkly at each gold star that went

up. Oliver said that he thought they were giving Rosie far too much attention, and for once Alice thought he had a point.

7

Vegetable Rhymes and Musical Fruit

"What are you going to be in the Christmas play, Rosie?" asked Mom one morning.

"A bamana," sang Rosie. "Sing the banama song, I'm a banama, all day long."

"Oh dear," said Dad.

"Not a very good choice," said Mom.

"She can't say the word properly!" said Oliver, who liked to point out the obvious.

"Bamana!" said Rosie.

"What's Hollyflower?" asked Alice. "A cauliflower?"

Rosie looked offended and said that Hollyflower was a brussels sprout. "Leafy greeny brussels sprout, dig a hole and pull me out. Three fat strawberries sitting in a row, water us and watch us grow. I'm a bamana, sing this song, I'm a danama all day long."

Alice suddenly had a feeling she knew what was coming next.

"Alice," said Mom.

"Yes?" said Alice.

"Rosie can't say the word 'banana' properly. And she has to be a banana and sing the bamana song, in the Christmas play."

"The bamana song?"

"I mean the *banana* song," Mom said hurriedly.

"Mmmm," said Alice.

"I don't suppose . . ." said Mom.

"Mmmm?" said Alice.

"Would you be a very very helpful girl and try to teach her to say it properly?"

Alice knew why she had been chosen. It was because until she was eight, she hadn't been able to say the word *animal* properly. It had always come out as *aminal*. It had become a bit of a family joke, especially with Oliver. And somehow she had learned to do it right in the end, and so they all thought she was the world's greatest expert at learning to say tricky words.

But teaching Rosie would be another matter altogether.

Rosie was the world's most awkward pupil. For one thing, she couldn't concentrate on anything for more than half a minute. For another, she much preferred to do things the wrong way. Alice had once been persuaded to try to teach Rosie the alphabet. Rosie believed she could read already and had her own names for all the letters. When Alice pointed to the letter "C," Rosie would explain kindly that it was called *hibok. Mercher, pogle, ploo,* she chanted, turning the pages. She would scamper off and stand on her head on the couch at the very sight of the letter "Y," which was called *groder* and which could only be viewed upside down. As for "X," she squealed and clapped her hands over her eyes at the very sight of it, which was called *plugg* and which made all the sparky ghosts that made machines work come whooshing out through the sockets in the walls if you dared to say its name. All in all it was hard to get anything done. By the end of the week Alice could spell her own name in Rosiespeak (*selendra, nimmo, vind, hibok, pogle*), and Rosie was carrying on just as before.

So she wasn't greatly hopeful about this new task.

"Is there a reward?" she asked. There was no point in being a very very helpful girl for nothing, if there was the slightest chance of getting paid for it.

Her parents had a brief whispered conversation, and then they told Alice they would pay her five dollars if Rosie said her lines perfectly on the day of the Humpty Dumpty Christmas Play.

Alice almost said yes right away. Five dollars was a lot of money. But then she stopped and thought.

"Ten dollars," she said.

Mom and Dad stared at her.

"It's the worst job you've ever asked me to do," said Alice. "It's not like cleaning your bedroom where you do it and it's done. It'll last for weeks and weeks. And however hard I try, I might get paid nothing at all! It's all up to Rosie in the end. And you know Rosie."

Her mom and dad looked at each other.

"Those are all very good points," said Dad.

"Ten dollars it is!" said Mom.

"We really want Rosie to get it right for the video," said Dad.

Mom gave a snort. "How much more money is that camera going to cost us?"

Dad winked at Alice. They had a deal.

* * *

Ten dollars was a *huge* amount of money.

"Say BA," Alice said to Rosie, for the twentieth time.

"BA!" said Rosie.

"BA!" said Hollyflower, who was nearly always present at the lessons.

"Say NA!"

"NA!" said Rosie.

"Say NA again!" said Alice.

"NA again!" said Rosie.

"Banana!" said Hollyflower. Alice stared sternly at her.

"Damama!" said Rosie.

Alice sighed. "Rosie, you're not trying."

"Am trying!" said Rosie.

"Now," said Alice, "take a deep breath."

Rosie took a great gulp of air and puffed her cheeks out.

"Empty your mind of everything except the word 'banana,'" said Alice.

Rosie looked doubtful.

"Now try," said Alice.

"Bamana," said Rosie, hopefully.

"Nearly right," said Alice. "But you always put an 'm' in it, Rosie. There aren't any 'm's in 'banana.' It's all 'n's. Think of all those 'n's."

Rosie screwed up her eyes in thought, though it was impossible to tell whether she was thinking about "n"s or something altogether different.

"Now," said Alice, "one last try. Ba-na-na."

"Nanana," said Rosie proudly.

"Banana," said Hollyflower, and Alice heaved a deep sigh.

"This isn't going to work," she said one day at breakfast. "I've been trying for three weeks now to teach her. All that's happened is that she's learned more ways of saying it wrong. Hollyflower thinks I'm crazy, and I've started to talk in vegetable rhymes."

"Never mind, Alice," said Dad. "You tried your best."

"It's only one more week until the Christmas play!" said Mom. "Oh, well. And she'd have made such a nice little pineapple."

"Sing the bamana song, all day long!" sang Rosie.

It had been just the same as usual. Rosie didn't learn a thing. The person actually affected by the lessons was Alice. All the rhymes and jingles chanted by Rosie and Holly were getting to her. She could hardly see a fruit or a vegetable any longer without making up a rhyme about it.

"Rotten orange, much too old, all my peel is stinky mold. Unripe apple, peel so thick, eat me up, I'll make you sick."

Rosie and Hollyflower thought this was

marvelous. They followed her around, begging for more. Alice started to feel like the Pied Piper.

"I didn't know you were a poet, Alice," her mom said. Alice was delighted. Perhaps at last she had found her special talent. She could be the family poet.

"Do *bean!*" said Rosie, chasing after her like a puppy nipping at her heels.

"Yes, do *bean!*" said Holly like a tiny tinkly echo.

Alice couldn't think of anything to say about a bean. Beans were boring. She did *onion* instead.

Rosie and Hollyflower giggled and said: "Now do *bean!*"

And all of a sudden Alice remembered a day at school when Jamie Logan in her class had said a rhyme about a bean that had made everybody laugh. How did it go again? "Hang on," she said, trying to focus on the memory. Beans, beans . . . Rosie and Hollyflower stood there looking at her expectantly. Beans, beans . . .

She had it!

"Beans, beans, the musical fruit. The more you eat, the more you toot!"

"Alice!" said Oliver.

"Alice!" said Mom, but her mouth was twitching with laughter. Rosie and Hollyflower had fallen over in a heap of laughter and appeared to be having fits. It took them a full five minutes to recover. Alice expected them to start asking her to do *lettuce,* but they seemed to have had enough of rhymes for the moment, and tiptoed away, whispering secretly to themselves.

8

Chance of a Lifetime

The day of the Humpty Dumpty Christmas play dawned crisp and clear. Dad was busy getting the video camera ready. The tape had to be wound to exactly the right place ready to start filming, and the battery had to be charged. He was supposed to have done this the night before, but he'd forgotten, and already Mom was tapping her foot in a way that meant *if that thing isn't ready soon, it's going to make us late and guess whose fault it will be? Not mine!*

"Can I tape it?" Alice asked. "Please?"

"Sorry, Alice," Dad said. "I've already promised Oliver."

"But Oliver did all the videotaping when we went to the zoo!" And a really dull video it had been, too. Oliver hadn't taken any shots of the family at all. His film had been one long series of bored animals standing around doing nothing. Some of the animals had been eating or playing before Oliver arrived, but for some reason at the sight of Oliver and the camera they all stopped. Quite a lot of them turned their backs and walked away. Oliver had recorded almost twenty minutes of this. Watching it was torture. Even Mom and Dad, who were never ever rude about anything made by one of their children, had struggled to stay awake through the whole thing, and Alice wouldn't be one bit surprised if one day soon they managed to tape over it by accident.

"It's not a question of taking turns, Alice. The video camera is not a toy."

Alice hated it when people told her, "it's not a toy," as if she wasn't old enough and smart enough to know for herself what was a toy and what wasn't. One of the problems with Oliver being so tall was that people treated him as almost grown-up and lumped Alice and Rosie together as "little ones," whereas in fact Alice was closer in age to Oliver.

"I've used the camera loads of times," she grumbled. She was allowed to practice at home, as long as nothing important was happening. "It's easy."

It *was* easy. There was a button for starting and stopping the recording, and a button for zooming in and out. Alice could find both those buttons without even looking. You had to remember not to jerk suddenly from side to side. And really that was all you needed to know. But Oliver had been promised already. It was hopeless.

They had to leave with the battery still only half-charged, and even so they were almost too late. All the seats were taken, and a whole row of dads were ready with their video cameras at the back, standing up and craning their necks to get a better view.

"I can only see half the stage!" said Oliver. "How am I supposed to make a video?"

"I can't see *any* of the stage," said Alice. Juliet, the youngest of the Humpty Dumpty teachers, heard this and came rushing over. "Don't worry!" she said brightly. "We've saved a row of chairs right at the front for little kids, and there's just one left! You come with me."

Little kids, thought Alice, offended. Really!

But then she had another, more interesting thought. She turned and looked at her father. Then she looked down at the video camera.

"Dad," she said.

"No!" said Oliver, seeing what was about to happen.

"But nobody except me will be able to see!" said Alice.

"It's true, Oliver," said Dad.

Oliver looked as if he was going to be sick. Even with a video camera, a preschool Christmas play was a fairly frightful place to be. Without one, you might as well die of embarrassment.

Alice hurried after Juliet, holding the camera carefully in both hands. The last empty seat was right in the middle of the front row, between two boys aged six or seven. They couldn't take their eyes off the video camera. "Wicked!" said the boy on the left. "Awesome!" said the boy on the right. They both sounded choked with envy. Alice glowed. This was the chance of a lifetime. Perhaps, if the video was perfect, they'd let her be the family film-maker in future. This would be far more fun than being the family poet.

Alice pressed the "record" button and shot some opening scenes. She filmed the curtain at the front of the room. A lot of squeaking and banging could be heard from behind the curtain. She stood up, turned around, and taped the audience. Some of the grownups waved, and the small boys in the front row made hideous faces. Alice stuck her tongue out at them.

There was a yelp from behind the curtain and a cry of, "Leave that beetroot alone!" Alice wheeled around slowly and took some shots of the walls, which were plastered with children's artwork. The pictures looked familiar, because children ages three and four always painted the same things. Bright yellow spiky suns. Boxy houses with doors in the middle and windows either side and chimneys with smoke coming out. Stick figure people with wild flyaway hair. And . . . an entire row of black splotches. Hang on a

minute. A row of *what?* Alice zoomed in for a closer look. The black splotches were labeled, "Big Black Blob by Rosie Singer."

It seemed darkly meaningful.

And then Carol, the teacher who'd made all the costumes, sat down at the piano and struck a chord. It was time for the show.

9

Jingle Beans

The audience fell silent. Amanda, the head teacher, stepped forward, cleared her throat and said, "Welcome, everyone, to our Christmas play! As you know, instead of the more traditional Nativity play, we at Humpty Dumpty have put together a little play to celebrate the meaning of this very special time of year with fruits and vegetables!"

There was a general low murmuring. "It's not really the same," muttered the woman sitting behind Alice.

Carol played another, more dramatic chord, and the curtain was pulled back to reveal three rows of wriggling fruits and vegetables. At the front, seven tiny red fruits were crouched on the ground as if they were hiding. At the back were the tall ones: the pineapple, the cucumber, the string bean. The middle row contained a dazzling variety of produce: a tomato, a pumpkin, a brussels sprout, and, on the very far left, a banana.

"Awwwwww!" cooed the audience adoringly.

Alice zoomed in on Rosie, who was standing quite still. The costumes covered the children from head to foot. All you could see of them were their little round faces peeking out through the face-holes Carol had made, and their chubby little arms sticking out through arm-holes in the sides. The poor string bean at the back didn't even have arm-holes, and was completely trapped inside its costume.

And so although Alice did her best to get a close-up of Rosie, really all that could be seen was banana. The woman behind her had noticed the same thing. "Lovely costumes they are, but I must say I'd rather be able to see the children's heads. If I didn't know which was mine, I wouldn't be able to tell!"

"My Holly's the brussels sprout," a familiar voice whispered back. "She was chosen to do the watering!"

"My Matthew's the green pepper," said the first voice, sounding very slightly crushed.

Carol launched into a tune, and the children sang, "Scatter seeds upon the earth, celebrate a baby's birth!"

The tomato picked up a pot and sprinkled the front row with something glittery. All the tiny strawberries and cherries rose to a kneeling position, waving their arms in the air.

"Awwwwwww," sighed the audience.

Alice had remembered to zoom back out for this scene, although the whole fruit and vegetable Christmas theme was starting to seem so funny that it was all she could do to hold the camera still. Any moment they might start singing "Jingle Beans" or "Once in Royal David's Turnip," and if that happened she was in serious danger of losing control altogether.

The children in the middle row started to say their rhymes. Rosie, on the far left, would be the last. *Banana,* Alice said inside her head, trying to beam the words across to Rosie by sheer force of will. *Banana.* You can do it. You know how you love to surprise people. Get it right for the very first time, live on stage. That would be a huge surprise! *Banana!*

The watermelon managed to say its lines correctly and so did Matthew the green pepper, causing a stifled sob of emotion from Mrs. Green Pepper in the seat behind Alice. The pumpkin forgot its second line, and the tomato was too overcome by the occasion to speak at all.

There were three more to go before Rosie.

Alice could feel her heart thumping as her sister's turn came nearer. In Rosie's place, she would be feeling more and more nervous as each child took his or her turn and the spotlight moved closer. Her throat would be drying up. She would be worrying that she wouldn't remember her lines, and that even if she did remember them, nothing would come out of her mouth but a hoarse whisper.

But Rosie was never nervous. Rosie had never

been afraid of anyone or anything in her entire life.

Alice noticed that a disturbance had broken out in the back row. The bean without arm-holes had lurched dangerously to the left, setting the beetroot wobbling into the celery, which in turn crashed into the cucumber, which went tumbling. The bean bounced back and knocked over the pineapple. Juliet and Amanda rushed on-stage like a couple of grocery clerks rearranging the produce after the customers have left a mess. Alice filmed it all.

"Now, children," Amanda hissed. "Remember what we practiced? If anything goes wrong, we just try to carry on as if nothing had happened! Where were we, then? The brussels sprout!"

Hollyflower stepped forward and piped: "Leafy greeny brussels sprout, dig a hole and pull me out!"

Mrs. Fowler wept.

And then, at last, it was Rosie's turn.

The banana shuffled forward. It seemed reluctant to take its turn, and the little that could be seen of the face in the banana costume had none of Rosie's usual spirit. Her mouth barely opened as she half-spoke, half-whispered: "I'm a banana all day long. Now let's sing the banana song."

She had done it! Rosie had said the word "banana" perfectly. Twice. Alice had earned her ten dollars!

And yet, as the children's high wobbly voices began to warble the Banana Song, the main thing Alice felt was disappointment. Rosie had gotten the words right, but she had sounded so dull and quiet! She had sounded nervous, even. Rosie, who had never feared anything in her life! What was happening? They had killed Rosie's imagination by calling it lies, and at the same time they had taken away the magic spark that made her special. Soon she would be exactly like any other four-year-old. And Alice didn't want that. Even if it made Alice seem dull and ordinary, she wanted her little sister back the way she always had been. What had they done? Why didn't anyone *understand?*

"Holly's going to do the watering now!" came a fiercely proud whisper from behind.

Hollyflower picked up a watering can. Alice, zooming closer, noticed two things about the watering can that were somewhat strange.

The first thing was that it seemed very heavy. It was quite a struggle for Holly to pick it up.

The second thing was that someone had removed the sprinkler from the end of the spout.

Holly lifted the can above the head of the strawberry kneeling on the far left and poised it in the pouring position.

"Water us and watch us grow!" sang the strawberries, and at that very moment a thick black liquid began to stream out of the watering can's spout, completely drenching the left-most strawberry. The strawberry gave a shocked little yelp and started to wail. Hollyflower made her way along the line, carefully pouring the liquid onto every single cherry and strawberry, staining the bright red costumes black and making gunky pools of blackness in their laps. The little faces blinked and crumpled in distress. The liquid flowed on down to the stage, forming puddles and rivulets that cascaded outwards to the front row of the audience.

There were squeals of alarm all around and calls to the children in the front to watch their shoes. Nobody knew what the black liquid was, but it looked nasty.

Alice lifted her feet off the floor, but she didn't stop filming for one second.

Panic had spread among the little cherries and strawberries, most of whom were now screaming at the top of their lungs. Moms and dads rushed forward to pick them up and comfort them. All their clothes were instantly ruined.

The children remaining on the stage stood frozen and bewildered as if glued to the spot. And then the bean splashed its way forward, spattering yet more black liquid, and took up a position in the center. There was a sudden hush as people realized that something more was about to happen. And then the bean announced, in a voice that chimed loud and clear:

"Beans, beans, the musical fruit! The more you eat, the more you toot!"

Alice thought, "I know that verse." And then she thought, " . . . and I know that voice!" She couldn't make any sense of it, but one thing she knew for sure.

The string bean was Rosie!

Alice felt suddenly flooded with happiness.

Amanda, whose face and hair were streaked with black, was losing her cool. "Roseanna Singer!" she shouted. "That wasn't the rhyme you were supposed to say! Who taught you that?"

And Rosie said, in her most meek and innocent voice, "My sister Alice teached me. I always have to say the truth."

The pumpkin finally lost its footing and fell, setting off a chain reaction that toppled all the remaining fruits and vegetables.

Alice gave a gasp and hit the "stop" button, just as the curtain came crashing down.

10

Trainspotting for Beginners

People were still talking about the Humpty Dumpty Fruit and Vegetable Christmas play months afterwards.

Amanda explained to the Singers that Rosie and the bean had swapped places after the first week of rehearsals. "We couldn't let her be the banana. She couldn't even say the word!"

"Why didn't you *tell* us?" everyone asked Rosie, who gave the wordless shrug that meant, "You didn't ask!"

Finally Alice understood why they'd sewn up the arm-holes of the bean costume. They thought Rosie couldn't do any damage without the use of her arms. It was a reasonable mistake to make if you didn't properly understand Rosie.

Holly explained that although she could tell that the watering can had felt different, and she had certainly noticed the black stuff pouring out of it, Amanda had told them over and over again that if anything went wrong, they should carry on as if nothing had happened. "And I did carry on! I did!" said Hollyflower, gazing up with huge innocent eyes. It was impossible to be suspicious of anybody so very small. You might as well blame a doll.

And of course Rosie claimed just the same thing. Even as the stage flooded, Rosie had carried on. It had been an unhappy accident that the wrong bean rhyme had come out of her mouth. This can so easily happen in the stress of the moment, when you know two bean rhymes! But she had tried to save the show. She had done her very best!

The thick black liquid in the watering can turned out to be paint. A huge amount of black powder paint had been mixed with water and glue. Nothing that was touched by this mixture was ever the same again.

And nobody found out for sure who was responsible.

It was certainly true that Rosie had become very attached to black paint in the weeks before the play. All her pictures had been big black blobs. She hadn't used any other color since October.

But, as usual, nothing could be proved.

Alice's video of the Christmas play grew into a local legend. It wasn't just because she'd had a perfect view of the stage. None of the dads at the back had had the sense to carry on filming once the catastrophe began. Every single one of them had dropped their camera or pressed "stop" or rushed up to the front to help. Alice was the only person who'd had the presence of mind to keep focused. Word got around that the little Singer child, the middle one, the one nobody usually quite remembered, had captured the whole event on video.

The Singer house began to seem like a private theater. All the other moms and dads made arrangements to come and watch the video. Soon they began bringing friends who didn't even have children at Humpty Dumpty, but had heard about it and wanted to watch it anyway. The friends brought their children and their children brought their friends.

Alice was in heaven. She made microwave popcorn, and Rosie and Hollyflower gave it out to the audience in paper cups. It was like having a party every single day.

Oliver would have nothing to do with any of this. He sat on his own out in the kitchen, writing headings and drawing lines in his Trainspotter's Log Book. The very mention of the words *video* or *camera* or *tape* made him freeze with fury.

It was all very unfortunate. The tape had been lined up at the wrong place before the play, and so Alice had recorded on top of Oliver's film of the zoo, erasing it forever. Only the last five minutes remained.

"Awfully sorry, Oliver," Dad said. "But these things do happen. It's very easy to do by accident."

Oliver just sniffed, and drew another line. He wanted nothing more to do with video cameras.

He had made that quite clear. If videotaping was going to be a free-for-all where even his baby sister was allowed a turn, then he, Oliver, was going to take up a more mature and interesting hobby. Trainspotting might, he felt, be the most exciting thing that had ever happened to him. It was a slight drawback that they lived fifteen miles from a railway station. He wouldn't actually be able to spot any trains for several years. But this was not, somehow, the point. In the meantime he had many glorious years of drawing perfectly straight lines with finely sharpened pencils to enjoy. When the time came to go out in search of trains, he would be properly prepared with an entire library of log books, blank except for his beautifully drawn lines. It would almost be a shame to spoil them with train numbers.

Alice had a few things she wanted to say to her parents. She called a private meeting.

"Dad, that wasn't true, what you said to Oliver about me recording over his video by accident. You put the tape at that place on purpose.

You knew exactly what you were doing. I *saw* you."

Her father looked shifty. "It was for everyone's good," he said. "If we'd had to sit through the zoo film again, someone might have started screaming aloud with the pain of it. Oliver would have been so terribly hurt. This way he never had to know."

"You *lied,*" Alice said relentlessly.

Her parents exchanged uncomfortable glances.

Mom said, "It's not wrong to lie to save hurting someone's feelings."

"And you tell Rosie it's her bedtime when it isn't."

Her parents wriggled awkwardly.

"All parents do that!" said Dad. Alice gazed at him sternly, as if to say, "Is that the best you can do?"

Mom seemed to get the point. "Okay, not everyone is as strict about lies as we've been with Rosie," she said.

Alice nodded. And she explained to them how

she was quite certain that Rosie behaved much better when she was allowed to tell stories.

"I think you're right," Dad said glumly. "But it's too late now. We can't just change our minds and go back on everything we've told her."

Mom sighed. "That's right, Alice. We can't suddenly say it's all right to tell stories after all."

"You may not have to," said Alice. "I've got an idea."

But before she could say another word, the doorbell rang.

11

Safety Pigs

The front door opened to reveal Mrs. Fowler and Holly, who had brought a party of eight to see the afternoon showing of the Christmas play video. Everyone except Oliver leapt into action right away. Rosie hurtled down the stairs, Dad put the tape in, Mom made drinks, and Alice scrambled to the microwave with the popcorn.

"We should start charging admission fees!" Dad said, dazed, at the end of the show.

"I'll tell you what you should do," said a woman who was a friend of a friend of the parents of Matthew the Green Pepper. "You should send it in to that TV show, *Honey, I Shot the Kid!*"

"We should what?"

"That's a good idea!" said Mrs. Green Pepper,

joining them. "You must have seen it. People send in home videos of their children, and they air the best ones. I've been watching it for six years, and I've never seen anything as good as what your Alice made."

Mom and Dad looked doubtful.

"They pay two hundred and fifty dollars for every one they use," the first woman said.

"What was the address again?" said Dad, grabbing a pencil and paper.

He made a copy of the tape and sent it in to *Honey, I Shot the Kid!* the very next day.

"Do you really think they'll show it on television?" Alice asked a hundred times. It was almost too exciting a thought to bear. She raced down to check the mailbox every morning for a month, but there was nothing from South Eastern TV, and gradually all her hope drained away. It surely wasn't possible that anybody would take longer than a month to answer a letter. They must have thrown the letter and the tape in the trash. This thought made her feel all crushed inside.

But then, one day in March, a letter arrived.

The people at *Honey, I Shot the Kid!* had been very impressed with the Singer video. They loved it! And they wanted to use it in the very first show of the next series. Not only that, but as the date drew near, they used it as the trailer. Twice every evening on prime time TV, Rosie, unrecognizable inside her bean costume, could be heard saying, "My sister Alice taught me!"

Alice was suddenly famous. People pointed her out in school. So many people knew her from watching the video at her house over Christmas that people even pointed her out in the street. For a few days she went around glowing, lit up by fame. It really did make you feel quite different.

But, somewhat to her surprise, she found that she didn't mind when it died down. All the attention had started to make her feel as if she was showing off. It had been fantastic fun to be a star for a week, but she didn't have the kind of personality that wants to be center stage forever. Rosie *did* have that kind of personality; she would always be the real star of the family. Alice knew that now. But Alice would be the one shooting the film. Which is very important. There wouldn't be any famous people at all, if there weren't other people behind the camera recording the film that made them famous.

Alice had completely forgotten about the two hundred and fifty dollars. But then one day in the mail a check arrived from South Eastern TV.

"Here's your two hundred and fifty dollars!" Dad said, tearing the envelope open and waving the check at her.

Everyone gasped.

"It's for *me?*" It was more money than Alice had ever dreamed of owning.

"You made the video!" said Dad.

"We'll open a savings account for you on Monday," said Mom.

"What a lucky girl!" said Mrs. Fowler, who had just arrived with Holly.

Alice blinked in confusion. Two hundred and fifty dollars was just too much money to keep for herself. It felt all wrong.

"Rosie should have some of it," she said. "It was because of her that everything went wrong and the video was funny. And whoever put the paint in the watering can," she added hurriedly.

"They never did find out which boy it was, but I have my suspicions about that pumpkin," said Mrs. Fowler. Mom and Dad nodded as if to say they'd thought much the same themselves.

Alice gave Rosie fifty dollars, and their parents opened a savings account for her, too.

She gave Oliver fifty dollars, to make up for taping over his zoo film, and because if only he'd been shorter, he might have filmed the Christmas tape himself. It wouldn't have been as good as Alice's, but there was no need for him to know that.

And Alice gave Dad fifty dollars for copying the tape and sending it to *Honey, I Shot the Kid!* — and for buying the video camera in the first place.

"I can't possibly take this," said Dad.

"In that case I'll have it!" said Mom, sharply. "It's about time I saw some money back from that camera!"

In the end Mom and Dad put this fifty dollars in the Disneyland fund, which now only needed

another sixty before there was enough money for the whole family to go.

Alice kept one hundred dollars for herself, which felt just about right.

But the best thing of all was that, bit by bit Rosie returned to her normal self. Strange things began happening again at Humpty Dumpty. Buttery sausagey slugwiches, magic beans, and tiger biscuits started to creep onto the menu. Plastic ghosts arrived to give the children invisible dancing lessons, and the Easter egg monster in the secret room had a particularly bad spell of behavior, eating several children for its lunch one rainy Tuesday, with microwave spangled poppycorns for dessert.

And every day that Rosie reported a menu of roast safety pigs and buttonberries, or camel relay racing, or outings to the North Pole, Mom and Dad would shake their heads in despair, tell her she was a dreadfully bad child, and stick a big black blob on Rosie's Truth-Telling Chart. They got some special skull and crossbones stickers for the most fantastic lies of all. Rosie *loved* the skull and crossbones stickers.

Everyone was content with this arrangement.

It had been such a strange time. Alice had lost her sister, got her back again, been on television (sort of), been famous (briefly), made a hundred dollars and given away a hundred and fifty. And for spring break, they were all going to Disneyland.

Alice would be making the family Disneyland video. She had been elected family film-maker forever. And her mother had promised never to say, "Boys and their toys!" ever again.

Life was very good indeed.